ONE STORMY NIGHT

For Daisy and Rose
Riordan

A Red Fox Book

Published by Random House Children's Books
20 Vauxhall Bridge Road, London SW1V 2SA

A division of Random House UK Ltd
London Melbourne Sydney Auckland
Johannesburg and agencies throughout the world

© Ruth Brown 1992

1 3 5 7 9 10 8 6 4 2

First published in Great Britain by Andersen Press Ltd 1992
Red Fox edition 1994

Printed in Hong Kong

RANDOM HOUSE UK Limited Reg. No. 954009

ISBN 0 09 929891 0

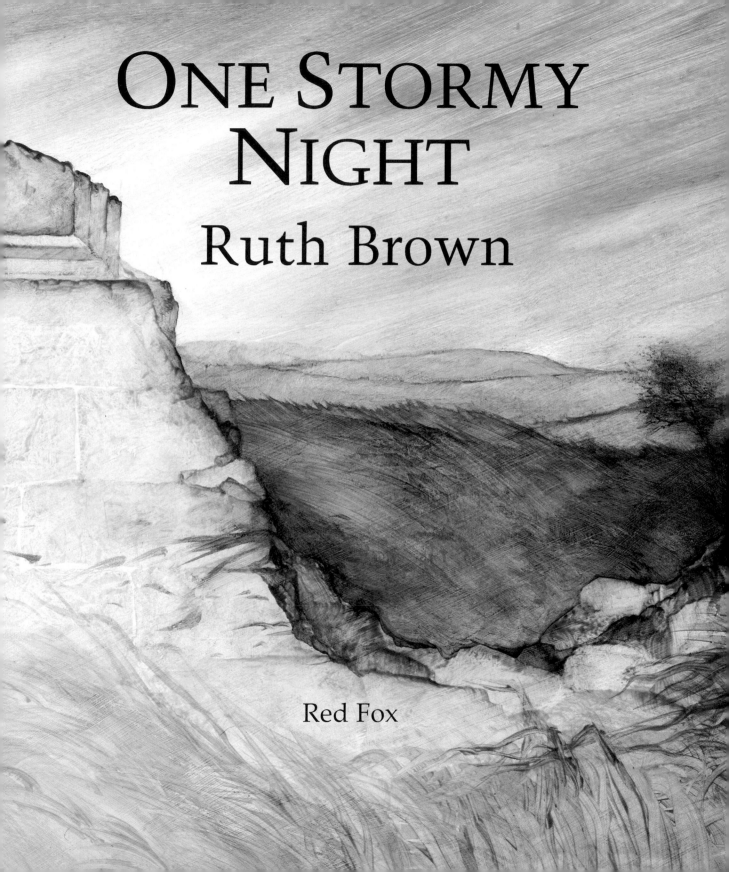

ONE STORMY NIGHT

Ruth Brown

Red Fox

One stormy night, the wind was howling,

the iron gate creaked,

and the black cat hissed.

Inside the house,
the fire-light flickered,

and, roused from his sleep,
the old dog barked.

The great oak door of the barn flew open.

The grey mare neighed

and a white owl screeched.

Then, just before dawn, the wind fell silent,
a bright star shone and the sky was clear.

For some a new day was beginning.

But others slept on,

in the morning sun.

Some bestselling Red Fox picture books

THE BIG ALFIE AND ANNIE ROSE STORYBOOK
by Shirley Hughes
OLD BEAR
by Jane Hissey
OI! GET OFF OUR TRAIN
by John Burningham
DON'T DO THAT!
by Tony Ross
NOT NOW, BERNARD
by David McKee
ALL JOIN IN
by Quentin Blake
THE WHALES' SONG
by Gary Blythe and Dyan Sheldon
JESUS' CHRISTMAS PARTY
by Nicholas Allan
THE PATCHWORK CAT
by Nicola Bayley and William Mayne
MATILDA
by Hilaire Belloc and Posy Simmonds
WILLY AND HUGH
by Anthony Browne
THE WINTER HEDGEHOG
by Ann and Reg Cartwright
A DARK, DARK TALE
by Ruth Brown
HARRY, THE DIRTY DOG
by Gene Zion and Margaret Bloy Graham
DR XARGLE'S BOOK OF EARTHLETS
by Jeanne Willis and Tony Ross
WHERE'S THE BABY?
by Pat Hutchins